MAR 0 4 2014

VERNON AREA PUBLIC LIBRARY DISTRICT

P9-BZC-669

For Sloan and Jane, the sweet little
girls who inspired this story. –T.B.

For my dad, for fixing everything for me. –S.M.

tiger tales
an imprint of ME Media, LLC
5 River Road, Suite 128, Wilton, CT 06897
Published in the United States 2013
Text copyright © 2013 Tilda Balsley
Illustrations copyright © 2013 Shelagh McNicholas
CIP data is available
ISBN-13: 978-1-58925-118-2
ISBN-10: 1-58925-118-0
Printed in China
SD10712
All rights reserved
1 3 5 7 9 10 8 6 4 2

For more insight and activities,
visit us at www.tigertalesbooks.com

Soo's Boo-Boos

She's Got 10!

by Tilda Balsley

Illustrated by
Shelagh McNicholas

tiger tales

VERNON AREA PUBLIC LIBRARY
LINCOLNSHIRE, IL 60069

Soo counted boo-boos.

"I've got 10!"

"Poor you," said Mom.
"Let's count again."

"Number **1** is bad, just wait. You see, my elbow isn't straight.

And let me show you boo-boo **2**.

My big toe rubs inside my shoe.

Remember when I skinned my knee?

The scab still itches. That makes **3**.

Number **4** is my chapped lips,

And number **5**, my nose, it drips.

6 boo-boos if you count my hair.
My ponytail feels tight up there.

My tongue is **7**. It feels awful!
I burned it on a toaster waffle.

8 is a mosquito bite.

I got it in the yard last night.

I pinched my finger in the door.

That's number **9** and here's one more!

10–a scratch about to bleed.
Some boo-boo help is what I need."

Mom smiled at Soo. "Just count on me.
Your boo-boos are my specialty.

This will fix that
scratch, I think,

What color do
you want—hot pink?

Does **10** feel better?
It looks nice!

For **9**, your finger, we'll rub ice.

And **8**, a mean mosquito bite.

Needs a kiss to make it right.

For number **7**, here's the trick.

To cool your tongue, just take a lick.

With number **6**, you need a hand?

Let's loosen up that rubber band.

For boo-boo **5**,
a nose that's yuck,
Here's a tissue.
We're in luck.

And this for chapped lips,
number **4**,

A cherry flavor
you'll adore.

Sweet-smelling lotion for your knee

And scabby boo-boo number **3**.

Your toes are scrunched and bunched, you say?

You're getting bigger every day.

New shoes for boo-boo number **2**.
Now just 1 elbow bothering you. . . .

Let's take this nifty scarf I've got
And make a sling. I'll tie the knot."

"We did it, Mom. Hooray, hooray!
All done with boo-boos for today.

So long! I'm going
out to play."

VERNON AREA PUBLIC LIBRARY
LINCOLNSHIRE, IL 60069

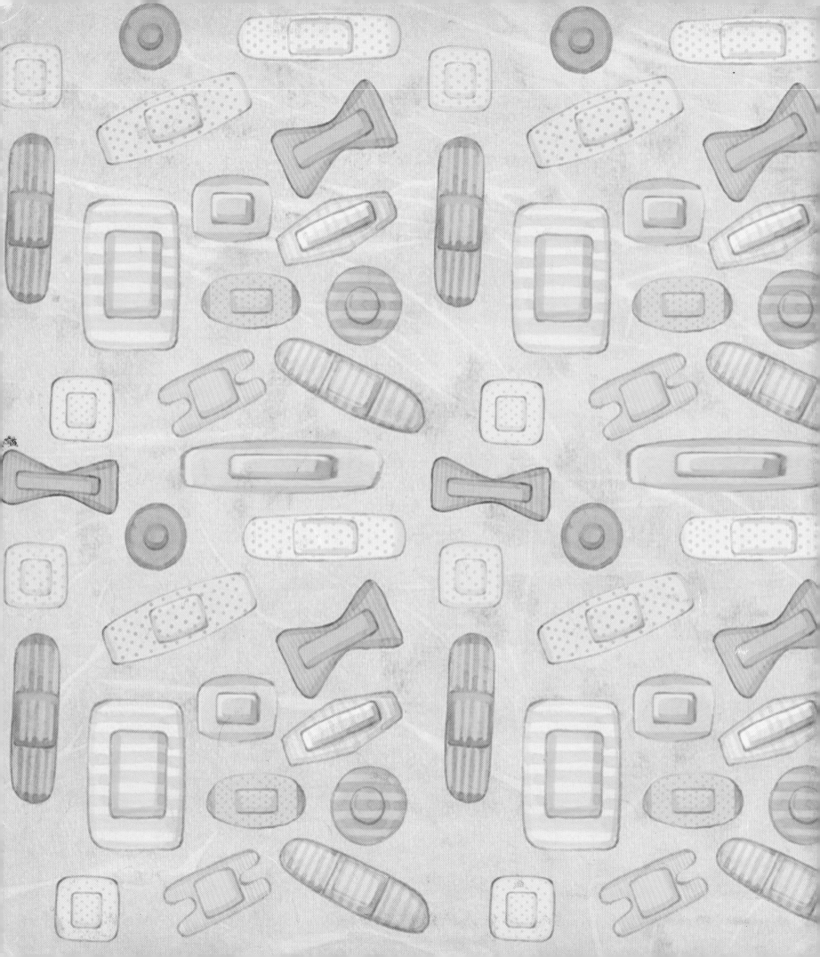